Adventures of Muku

by Geraldine E. Nicholson

Dillon Press, Inc.
Minneapolis

illustrated by Carolyn Lodge

BECAUSE THE FOLK TALES OF HAWAII should be considered as part of our national literature, I have woven several of them into the *Adventures of Muku*. I gathered much of my material from the University of Honolulu library during the time I spent there, and afterwards had the good fortune to receive advice and suggestions from Padraic Colum who had collected the ancient tales.

Muku is my own invention. But it seemed to me that a young reader would be able to identify with him. I've taken no other liberties with the fables.

GERALDINE E. NICHOLSON

39 50

©1975 by Dillon Press, Inc. All rights reserved

Dillon Press, Inc., 500 South Third Street
Minneapolis, Minnesota 55415

Printed in the United States of America

Library of Congress Cataloging in Publication Data

Nicholson, Geraldine E.
    Adventures of Muku.
    SUMMARY: Several Hawaiian folk tales concerning menehunes, or Hawaiian little people, are woven into the adventures of a fictional menehune, Muku.
    [1. Hawaii—Fiction.   2. Folklore—Hawaii]
I. Lodge, Carolyn, ill.   II. Title.
PZ7.N552Ad   [Fic]   74-34434
ISBN 0-87518-086-8

Contents

1. Muku Arrives in the World

LONG AGO, when the world was much younger than it is now, a strange race of little people shared the islands of Hawaii with humans of normal size. They called themselves men-e-hu-nes, and so great were their numbers that they could build a dam or a bridge in a single night. "Pau," they would say when a work was finished. But if at sunrise it had not been completed, thus it remained for all time.

Since the humans went about the islands only in the daytime, and the menehunes only at night, generations of both races might live and die without any knowledge of each other. Most menehunes had no idea that anyone was bigger than they were. Two feet was their average height. That was bigger than the lizards scuttling through the grass, bigger than the hoot owls in the trees, and even bigger than the rats nesting in the thickets. "And that," said the menehunes, "is big enough to be."

The menehunes thought that they were very handsome people. Their shoulders were broad, their legs sturdy, and the skin on their ears and noses was the rosy pink of a pickled shrimp. Only on ears and noses did skin ever show. Every menehune arrived in the world with a nice soft coat of down which covered him from the top of his head to the tips of his toes. As he grew, and he lost no time doing that, the down turned into silky black hair. This kept him warm on chilly days, dry when the rains came, and comfortable all the time. No menehune had to worry about clothes. The only suit that he would ever need came with him.

The chief of the menehunes was the tallest of them all. His name was Nai-pu-al-e-hu, and he was a full three feet. Even when the other menehunes stretched their spines until they were ready to snap, few of them could lift their heads above Nai-pu's chin.

The menehunes loved their chief, and at his command, they dragged smooth stones from the beach or rolled boulders from the mountain. They had all the time in the world to get ready, but only one night to build.

Between the menehunes and the other forest creatures,

there was a bond of mutual trust. The menehunes might never harm a living creature, and no creature, great or small, could harm them. The owls, wisest of all the forest folk, were their special friends, and they were pleased when Nai-pu asked them for advice. Secretly, the owls thought the menehunes were very silly to eat only raw fish and fruit when plump young rats were so much more tasty. But they were glad it was so. For their own protection, the Owl King had made his subjects take an oath that never, under any condition, would they leave the grove he governed, and they knew how rapidly the rat supply would dwindle if the menehunes ever acquired a taste for them.

In all of this peaceable kingdom, Nai-pu alone was unhappy. More than anything else in the world, he wanted a son who would carry his name and add to his fame. This favor the gods had denied him. Three daughters had been born to him, but no son.

"Heaven is playing a joke on me," Nai-pu thought to himself. "Surely my next child will be a boy."

But when in due course, the fourth child was presented to him, she, too, was a girl. Nai-pu looked down on her puckered little red face and groaned in his misery.

Ka-u-ki-u-ki, who was Chief Adviser to great Nai-pu, looked at his lord in astonishment. But since he could give advice only when it was called for, he said no word.

Nai-pu groaned again, "Why must every child be a female?"

The Chief Adviser answered gravely, "Without females, my lord, we would have no menehunes at all. They are the mothers of the race."

"What you say is true. But how can I provide royal weddings for so many?"

"They must have royal weddings only if they are princesses, my lord." replied Ka after some thought. "Could you hide this last child or disguise her in some way?"

"I can do much better than that. This child will rise higher than any royal princess. Fly from my sight, Mimo! Build a nest and be happy. Be a mynah bird!"

The next moment, as though touched by a magic wand, the unwelcome little menehune changed her arms for wings and flew away.

When his fifth daughter was born, Nai-pu sighed in dismay and said to himself, "Three royal weddings are more than enough! Since I gave the sky to one princess as her birthright, I'll give water to this one. She will live as a turtle, at home in a fishpond or the ocean. Her name shall be Tina."

High above, in the dark shelter of leafy branches, the owls blinked their yellow eyes and stretched their necks for a glimpse of the unhappy babe her father had refused to accept.

The fifth daughter was growing a shell. First her head, then her arms and legs, and finally the rest of her disappeared beneath it. Then she slid off the ti leaf, landed with a plop, and waddled off to the fish pond.

At last one night, when the moon pressed her chin against a hau tree, a son was born to Nai-pu. At the good news, he leaped in the air and shouted with delight.

"I must see him at once," he cried. "Bring me my wonder child, my mighty little warrior!"

At that command, all the menehunes lined up on either side of his throne until they formed an aisle a mile long. Then in tribute, an owl perched upon every shoulder, its yellow eyes lighting the way for the bearer. Far along the line he came with the youngest and most welcome menehune cradled on a ti leaf. Every neck was craned for a glimpse. But as the bearer passed, a strange thing happened. No happy smiles greeted Nai-pu, and the moon fled away from the hau tree.

The chief stiffened on his throne. "What is happening here?" he cried in a thunderous voice. "Come faster, come faster, I must see for myself!"

The bearer quickened his pace and soon stood trembling before the great Nai-pu. Then he fell on his knees and held out the ti leaf cradle. When the chief saw the little creature upon it, he screamed like a wild thing in a trap.

"What is this squirming red lizard you've brought me? My son? I couldn't bait a minnow with a thing so small! Where is his hair? Is he wearing a shell? Look at him, look at him, he's as bare as a bone!"

The nearest menehunes looked. The tiny one on the leaf had stopped squirming and now he stretched as far as he could. But even so, he was small indeed, hardly the length of his father's hand and smooth as the palm of it. As the other menehunes crowded closer to see him, so many tears splashed on the ti leaf that Nai-pu snatched up his son in alarm.

"Get back, get back! Are you trying to drown him? He's not the son I prayed for, but he's the only one I have and I want him alive!"

High above, in the dark shelter of leafy branches, the owls shook their heads in puzzlement. Could it be that the great chief was losing his magic powers? The great birds stretched their necks for another glimpse of the father and his child.

The youngest menehune gave a squeal like a frightened mouse as his father hugged him to his hairy chest. Then Nai-pu laughed loud and long.

"You see? Small though he is, he can speak for himself. I must find a proper name for him."

"He's no bigger than a minute," hooted one of the owls. "Call him Muku."

"I *will* call him Muku. As you say, Wise One, Muku means a minute. But it also means the distance from my fingertips to my other elbow. Let him grow to *that,* and I will be content. The gods must have a reason for sending me such a son. I dare not change him. Who knows what he will do when the time comes!"

"Not much," sneered the owl. "With no hair to cover him, he will die of exposure."

"Not if I can help it!" yelled Nai-pu.

"We'll save a few feathers for him when we moult," jeered another owl.

"You have broken the bond of our friendship. You shall pay for this insult!" raged Nai-pu.

But the insolent owls shrilled back at him, "Who, who, who?" and flew off to their nests. Their feud with the menehunes had begun.

2. Mimo and the Jealous Sisters

YOUNG MUKU STARTED LIFE in a cradle made of a coconut shell. This was slung between two bamboo shoots so that it would sway back and forth with the breeze. But the bamboo shoots grew so fast that one night when his mother went to look at him, Muku and his cradle were high above her head! After that, two steady breadfruit saplings supported the cradle, and Muku slept through the days in their thin-leafed shadow. But at night he was just as much awake as anyone. No sensible menehune ever opened an eye when the sun was out. All their work was done at night.

As soon as the moon rose, Nai-pu was sure to make his son a visit. Then Muku would nibble his finger, and wrinkle his little red button of a nose to show his father that he loved him. This made the three sisters who were supposed to care for their baby brother very jealous.

"Our father never looks at our fine coats," said the eldest, "but he loves that little hairless one. We'll fix him!"

After that they took turns poking Muku, pinching him,

and pulling his nose. When he cried, they would run and hide.

"Such a bad-tempered baby!" his mother would say. But Tina the turtle, and Mimo the mynah bird, found out what the sisters were doing and decided to watch over their little brother. The next time a jealous one tiptoed to Muku's cradle to pinch him, Mimo flew at her head, and Tina snapped at her big toe.

"Oh!" she cried, hopping on one foot and holding her throbbing toe. "Why do you protect the little hairless one? Our father loves him best because he is a boy!"

"Do all of you believe that?" Mimo asked the three. The eldest sister hung her head in shame. "No," she whispered. "Our father loves him best because there is only one of him and three of us."

"Then if you would please your father, never hurt him again," snapped Tina. "Promise me that because Mimo and I would rather be your friends than your enemies."

"Oh we will, we will!" the sisters cried, fearful of the anger of Mimo and Tina, but still they felt no love for their little brother.

When the sisters were sent to feed Muku, Mimo perched near by. She saw them hold out a bit of banana, but before the baby could get it, they would pop it into their own mouths! From that time on, Mimo stayed close to the coconut cradle at feeding time and pecked at their fingers until they promised to give Muku every bit of his dinner.

So in spite of the jealous sisters, Muku did grow. But, sad to say, when his head was as far from his heels as Nai-pu's fingertips were from his other elbow, Muku was still the smallest of the menehunes and the least protected. Every scorpion or centipede could bite him at will, and the least breeze made him shiver.

One night when Muku was crying miserably, Mimo flew from her nest and called to their mother.

"Mother," said she, "my poor little brother will surely die unless we find some way to protect him. Make him a coat of banana leaves and see how that will do."

The mother called her daughters at once and told them to look for the softest banana leaves with the prettiest fringes. But the daughters brought back only those that were dry and coarse. When the coat was made and fitted on poor Muku, it prickled and scratched until he was in torment. At last he tore it off and threw it into the fish pond.

The jealous sisters, who were hoping he would do this very thing, were overjoyed. They couldn't wait to go racing off to tell their father what his darling son had done. When they found the chief, their little eyes were sparkling, and their red noses were shining like Christmas tree bulbs.

Nai-pu was playing dominoes with Ka-u-ki-u-ki. He had a beautiful set which his workers had carved from coral. But when he heard what the daughters had to tell him, he cried out in a rage, "Of course Muku tore his coat off when it scratched him. I would have done the same thing myself. Now get out of my sight, you tattling oysters!"

Then he pelted them with dominoes until they fled screaming. The double six was never found.

Once again Muku had nothing to cover him. The watchful owls, delighting in what had happened, deliberately shed feathers around him, but after Nai-pu's stern warning, no one dared to make use of them.

"It isn't fair," Muku protested to Tina the turtle who had stopped by to see him. "Even the rats are better off than the son of Chief Nai-pu! Something must be done!"

Tina drew her head into her shell for a moment to think. Then she stuck it out again, looking very pleased with herself. "Go to Mimo. She is sure to help you. The coat was her suggestion in the first place, and I have no doubt she will have another. Mynah birds are full of ideas."

So Muku went to Mimo.

13

3.
Mimo's Wonderful Idea

MIMO WAS BUSY hatching some eggs when Muku found her, so she had plenty of time to listen to his troubles and to what Tina had said. "Anybody has more ideas than a turtle," she sniffed, tilting her yellow beak and eyeing the scratches on his legs. "You certainly need help. You're like an egg without a shell!"

"Look through the forest, Mimo," Muku begged her. "You may find some dead creature who no longer needs its fur coat."

"You couldn't wear that! But keep your eye on my youngest here, and I'll find something." Then off she flew.

She had not gone far before she heard sad sounds coming from a grass hut. Two young girls were weeping beside the body of an old man who was saying in a weak voice, "I should have lived much longer if we had no rainy season, and the nights were as warm as the days. Now I am about to die. But do as I tell you, my daughters, and I will provide for you. Bury my body beside the stream, and a mulberry tree, as yet unknown to man, will spring from it. Tear a strip of bark from the tree trunk and soak it in water. Then pound it to a pulp between two stones and you will have a piece of fine tapa cloth with which to clothe yourselves."

"This may be the answer to my search," thought Mimo. "I must see what happens."

The daughters buried their father, as he had told them to do, and almost at once a tree sprang from his grave. When the branches were above their heads, the girls cut a strip of bark from the trunk, soaked it in the stream, and pounded it between two stones. They pounded and pounded until Mimo grew quite dizzy watching them. But at last they had a fine piece of tapa cloth, and Mimo flew down to admire it.

"That brown and white pattern is really beautiful," she chirped. "May I have it, please?"

The startled sisters looked at her. "What?" said the elder. "Give our first piece of tapa cloth to a mynah bird? Go away, foolish creature!"

"It's far too small to clothe a human like yourself," Mimo answered reasonably. "But it would make a fine coat for my menehune brother Muku."

"No doubt it would," sniffed the younger sister, "but we mean to keep it for ourselves."

Mimo sighed. "Then I must tell everyone about your magic tree. By this time tomorrow, they will have every bit of bark stripped from its limbs."

The sisters looked at each other in dismay. "No, no! You must not do that!" said the elder. "This is our secret. Will you promise never to mention it to a soul if we give you the cloth?"

"May I lose all my feathers if I do!"

"Then take it. But mind you don't come back for more!"

Mimo promised, and the next moment she was flying back to Muku with the tapa cloth safe in her beak.

When Muku's mother saw what Mimo had brought, she sat down at once to make a little coat for her son. Her needle was a thorn, and her thread a strand of beach grass. The coat was so small that it took only a short time to make; and before the night was over, Muku was wearing it. All the menehunes gathered around to admire him, for the coat was beautiful.

Nai-pu asked Mimo to get him one. "After all," said he, "I am the chief of this tribe, and I am sure a red jacket would become me."

Mimo shivered in her feathers as he spoke, for she remembered her promise to the sisters. But she answered bravely, "I am sure you would look very handsome, Father, only it would be a pity to cover your glossy hair. There might even be people who would say you had lost it all and were as bare as Muku!"

Nai-pu thought over her words for a long while. He had always found it much more difficult to use his head than his hands. But at last he nodded agreement.

"You are right. I have hair." Mimo was so relieved that she took a cold bath in the fish pond.

After that, Muku wore his tapa coat every night and almost forgot he had ever been without it. Now he felt like a true menehune, and he added six stones to a wall the others were building. He had three more in readiness when dawn came.

"Too bad, young fellow," said Ka-u-ki-u-ki, one of the workers. "You can never add those stones to this wall. It isn't quite finished, but you know the menehune law. We can never go back to any task we cannot complete in one night."

Muku dropped his stones on the ground. The menehune law seemed very unfair to him. "When I am the chief, that's the first law I'll change!"

4.
Muku
and the
Baby Owl

BESIDES HIS JEALOUS SISTERS, Muku had other enemies he knew nothing about: the owls in the breadfruit trees. How scornfully they looked down on him!

"What kind of a chief is Nai-pu to have such a mouse of a son?" asked one in disgust. "See him strut about in his silly jacket. Why he couldn't grow a pin feather!"

"Nor even a tuft of hair," sneered another. "Why should we respect these menehunes? They aren't nearly so wise as we are."

The leader of the owls preened his plumage. "One of these nights soon we will have a showdown. Now we must take that jacket away from young Muku. He is far too full of his own importance. Come closer and hear my plan."

Then from every branch of every tree the owls came

crowding around their leader in a feathery huddle, and hooted with delight when they heard what he proposed to do.

One night, soon afterwards, when the wild orchids lifted their faces to the moon, Muku saw a young owl fall out of its nest. The poor little thing began to flutter along the ground crying bitterly. Muku's heart was filled with pity.

"Don't cry," he said. "I'll put you back in your nest." He stooped to pick the bird up, but he hopped just beyond Muku's reach.

"You don't understand," he told Muku tearfully, "I've lost something and I must find it. Follow me and I will tell you about it."

So Muku followed the little owl. But he told his story one word at a time with three hops between each, and they were far into the forest before he finished.

"I've lost my father's wisdom stone in this lake," he moaned, squeezing still another tear from his yellow eyes, "and I can never find it again, for I can't swim!"

"What will happen if you don't find it?" Muku asked. He could swim, but the dark pool beneath the tangled vines looked very cold, and he hated to take off his tapa jacket.

"My father will drive me from the nest. He may even

kill me," the owl's yellow eyes blinked in fear. "I must have it back!"

"Then you shall," Muku promised, and without another word he slid out of his warm coat and dove into the pool.

Now it happened that his sister Tina was visiting a turtle friend in that very pool, and she heard all the owl had been telling him on the bank. The minute she saw Muku come gliding through the water she called out to him, "Go back, go back! The owl has tricked you, Muku! Go back! He is stealing your coat!"

Muku rose to the surface of the pool at once, but he was too late. The sad little owl had disappeared with his coat.

Tina crawled out of the water after him. "It is too late for me to help you this time, little brother. But if ever you need me again, throw three pebbles into the water, and I will come to your aid. If real danger threatens, throw five pebbles, and I will summon all of my turtle friends to help you."

Muku thanked her, but he could not imagine any greater misfortune than the loss of his coat. The air was warm and so were his tears, but he shivered. What would become of him now?

5.
The
Mud Hen's
Secret

ONCE AGAIN MUKU HAD NOTHING to protect him from the thorns and briars that seemed to spring up on all sides of him. But he was so angry at the young owl who had tricked him, that he hardly noticed his scratches or where he was going. Suddenly he found himself in a moonlit clearing before a fine bamboo house thatched with palm leaves. A young man stood at the door complaining to an old woman.

"It is true, Mother, that men call me Maui, the Hero, because I pulled this island out of the sea and lifted up the sky. I have even held back the sun with a coconut rope. But when a chill wind sweeps the island, I am as cold as anyone and every day I eat raw roots and fish like the poorest of people."

"All your troubles would be ended, my son, if you

could find out the secret of fire from the mud hen. The weather never bothers her or her young ones. She can start a nice cheerful blaze anywhere at all. Why won't she let the rest of us know how she does it? Why the gods should have entrusted such rare and precious knowledge to that foolish creature, I shall never understand! She's just a coot!"

The hero Maui frowned. "It is true," he agreed, "that the mud hen cooks her food and produces warmth when she pleases. But she is careful never to light her fire until my friends and I have gone fishing. How, then, can I learn her secret?"

His mother had no answer. But Muku, stepping out from beneath a guava bush which had concealed him, entered the conversation.

"I am only a menehune, great Maui," said he, "but I think I can help you."

The startled hero and Hina, his mother, looked down at him in amazement. Then Maui gave a great shout of laughter. "Look who has come to solve our problem, Mother! Speak up, sir, and give us the answer."

"First I must ask you a question," replied Muku modestly. "How many young men go fishing with you?"

"Three," answered Maui.

"And arc you thc first in the canoe?" Muku inquired.

"Certainly," Maui boasted. "I am the hero."

"Then here is what you must do. On the next trip, put a calabash on a stick and set it in your place."

"A calabash?" questioned Maui wonderingly. "How can a big gourd take my place in the boat?"

"Mud hens can never see well at a distance," explained Muku, "and she is sure to mistake the calabash for your head. Then she will think you have gone fishing with the others and start her fire."

"A splendid idea," declared Maui, snatching up a calabash his mother had set out to catch rain water. "Let us start at once."

At that moment Mimo lighted on a lantana bush beside Muku. "Just a minute," she chirped. "If this scheme works, we will expect a fire stick as a reward."

"This is Mimo, my bird sister," Muku explained to Maui. "I think she is right. I have lost my tapa coat and need some way to keep warm."

"You may have as many coals as you like," promised Maui, "but now I must hurry."

Muku and Mimo followed the hero as he ran down to the beach to tell the plan to his three friends. At last, with the calabash propped up on a stick to take the place of Maui's head, the boat was shoved into the water. Hidden away in the long marsh grass, Muku and

Mimo waited with Maui for the mud hen to count the fishermen. Soon she came scurrying along the beach and peered after them. With her near-sighted eyes she was sure she saw four men, so she called her children together.

"Thank goodness, the men have all gone fishing," said she. "Now I shall light a fire and broil bananas for breakfast."

At these words, all the little mud hens went flip-flapping after her to a sheltered spot on the beach. But Maui dared not leave his hiding place until the fire was kindled for fear the mud hen would refuse to light it if she saw him. When at last flames were leaping in the air, Muku breathed in his ear, "Now!" and they crawled out of the grass. The lovely smell of broiling bananas teased their nostrils as they drew near to the soaring

blaze around which the little mud hens were yip-yapping hungrily.

"Good morning, Mother Mud Hen," said Maui. "It seems we are just in time for breakfast."

"No, no!" squeaked the little mud hens in a panic. "That's our breakfast and you can't have it!"

"Then give me the secret of fire," replied Maui, "and you may keep your breakfast."

"Not while I live," stormed the mud hen. And, before anyone could stop her, she had brushed wet sand over the fire and put it out. "Now if you kill me, no one else will ever know my secret."

This threat stopped Maui for a moment. But Muku whispered, "She doesn't want to die and leave all her children!" And Mimo chirped, "Scare her!"

So Maui seized the mud hen and shook her until her little ones, who had hidden under her wings, ran this way and that in terror. Finally the mud hen gasped, "Rub the reeds together. There is fire in them." Maui stopped shaking her, but he did not let her go.

"You must come and show me," answered Maui cleverly, for he knew she was planning to run and hide. Holding her firmly under his arm, he picked two long reeds, but rub as hard as he could, no fire came from them.

"I should hate to shake you again," said he to the mud hen, putting his hands around her neck.

"Go to the taro," she told him weakly. "Rub those leaves together."

So Maui went to find taro leaves, but he took the mud hen with him and she didn't like it. No fire came from rubbing the taro.

"How could it?" thought Muku.

The stubborn mud hen was fluttering helplessly now, but once more Maui shook her, though gently. "The banana stumps," she murmured with her eyes closed, "Rub them together."

Maui rubbed the banana stumps with all his might, but not the smallest spark flew out to reward him. Then he held the mud hen at arm's length and shook her until her head hung limp and he shouted in a terrible voice, "Give me the secret or your children will have no mother!"

At his words, the frightened little mud hens came swarming around their mother and cried out, "Tell him, tell him!"

With what breath that was left to her, the mud hen gasped, "The bark of the hau and the sandal. Rub them together."

Maui dropped her then, for he knew she had told the

truth. This time flames leaped from the bark as he rubbed, and Muku piled twigs and dry grass on the sand to catch them. For a long time the three watched the wonder with delight.

"At last we have the secret of fire, Muku, thanks to your plan. And here, at the end of this stick, is the glowing ember that I promised you," said Maui.

"Give it to me," cried Mimo, "I will fly with it in my beak."

"You must hurry then," Maui warned her. "The fire won't stay at one end. It's a demon that devours what it touches!"

Mimo promised, and seizing the fire stick, flew high in the air. Muku was about to run after her when Hina called to him from the leafy shelter where she had watched Maui deal with the mud hen.

"Wait, Menehune! We owe you far more than a single coal from the secret fire. What other favor can we grant you?"

"Yes, yes," cried Maui, perching Muku on his broad shoulder. "Tell us your heart's desire and you shall have it."

Muku clutched at the hero's ear to balance himself as he answered sadly, "I just want to look like other menehunes. But no one in all the islands can help me to grow the hair which should cover me."

"I can," said Hina, taking a nut shell from her pocket. "This nut shell contains a precious ointment. Rub it on your legs, your arms, and all the rest of you. Then see what happens."

Too excited to speak, Muku slid from Maui's shoulder and took the nut shell from her hand. Then he smeared himself with the ointment.

"Now close your eyes and count to seven," Hina commanded.

Muku did as he was told. As he counted, Maui led him to a pool of clear water which reflected the moon. There Muku opened his eyes. To his complete astonishment, a strange little menehune stared back at him from the pool. Muku noticed especially that the strange menehune was covered from head to foot with the silkiest, shiniest coat of black hair he had ever seen. Muku blinked. The stranger blinked right back. Muku rubbed his nose in bewilderment. The stranger rubbed his nose. Baffled, Muku turned to Maui.

"Who. . . who is it?" he faltered.

"Who is it?" shouted Maui, "Why it's you!"

Muku looked down at his chest, his arms, his legs, and once again at his reflection. There was no doubt about it. He was the strange little menehune, clothed at last. What would his father say? What would everyone say? He couldn't wait to find out.

"Thank you, thank you, thank you!" he cried and darted off through the forest, leaving Maui and Hina smiling after him.

6.
Mimo
Refuses
a Reward

WHEN MIMO REACHED HOME after her flight through the forest, the fire had burned so far along the stick Maui had given her that there was hardly enough left to hold. She dared not drop it for fear of setting the grass and trees on fire, and so she flew on desperately until at last she set down her dangerous prize on a stone outside Nai-pu's door. Then she chirped feebly for help. The menehunes came running. They had never seen fire before, and their startled eyes mirrored the flame.

"This stone is too small," Mimo told them. "The fire must have room or it will go out. Bring me a great stone with a hollow in its heart. Then you shall see magic. Hurry, hurry!"

The menehunes scattered like leaves in the wind. Soon they had rolled a hollow rock from the hillside and filled it with dry grass as Mimo told them to do. Alas, the fire had burned to the very end of the stick, and Mimo could no longer pick it up.

"Save the fire!" she cried frantically. "We can't let it die now!"

"Of course we can't," agreed Nai-pu, and stepping forward, he picked up stone and all and dropped the fire into the hollow rock. Instantly bright tongues of flame leaped from the dry grass, and warmth reached out to the menehunes. At first they stood still in wonder. Then they crowded so close that spitting sparks singed their hair.

"Stand back!" Mimo warned them. "You may see it and feel it, but you may never touch this miracle."

At this moment, Muku, exhausted from running, came panting into the circle. As he had expected, no one recognized him at first. But when they had heard his story, the menehunes thought it was hardly less wonderful than the fire. Nai-pu held his son high in the air for all to see and admire. Then the menehunes cheered and cheered until they had awakened every echo on the island. A great feast was prepared. And, for the first time, chief and worker tasted broiled shrimps and baked bananas, delicacies which had been known before only to mud hens.

At last, when everyone was so stuffed with good food that skins threatened to burst, the precious fire was banked, and as the sun rose, the merrymakers trailed off to bed. Only Nai-pu was still wide awake, and suddenly he noticed what Muku had hoped would never come to his attention.

"Where is your tapa cloth jacket?"

"He doesn't need that any more," said Ka-u-ki-u-ki, who had heard the owls chuckling over the great joke they had played on the son of the chief.

"Maybe he doesn't, but what has become of it? Where is it, Muku?"

So, though from shame and sleep he could hardly hold his head up, Muku was forced to tell the whole sorry tale of the baby owl's trickery.

When he finished, Ka muttered angrily, "You wait! The villains shall pay for this outrage!"

To Muku's surprise, Nai-pu suddenly laughed and patted his hand. "What difference does it make now?

You have a coat nobody can steal." Then he turned to Mimo. "I realize now that I made a mistake when I changed you from a menehune to a bird, Mimo. As a reward for the great gift you have brought us, I wish to change you back again."

Mimo choked on a worm she was about to swallow. "Oh don't do that, Father!" she squawked in alarm. "I don't want to give up my wings!"

Nai-pu blinked in astonishment. "Why I should think that any animal would want the chance to be a mene-hune!"

"What use would I be to you as a menehune?" inquired Mimo shrewdly. "Could I have flown with the fire stick if I had been a menehune?"

Nai-pu turned her words over in his mind before he answered. "No, I suppose you couldn't have. And if you had walked, you might have burned up the whole island. But if you don't want to be one of us, what other favor may I offer you as a reward?"

Mimo sighed with relief. "Thank you, Father, you are very kind. I have nothing in mind at the moment. Please let me wait until I can think of something really worthwhile. Then I will tell you."

"Anything, Daughter, anytime," said Nai-pu grandly.

Lifting her tired wings, Mimo flew to her nest.

7.
The Fate
of Ka-u-ki-u-ki

ON THE NIGHTS THAT FOLLOWED, Muku was so pleased with his wonderful new coat that he spent half of his time admiring himself. As soon as the moon rose, he would look at his reflection in every pool he could find. He was still afraid, at the bottom of his heart, that one would show him the poor bare fellow he had been.

"See our young peacock strut!" Nai-pu chuckled one night as he and Ka watched Muku swaggering by. "You would think he was the first menehune who ever had hair! Let's follow him and have some fun."

As usual, Muku went straight to a pool and looked in, grinning at his reflection. The menehune in the pool grinned back. Muku raised his hand in salute. The other menehune returned it. Then, inspired, Muku stood on one leg and hopped.

"Now!" said Nai-pu to Ka, and together they gave a push.

Splash! The menehune in the pool ducked, and the next second, gasping and sputtering, Muku bobbed to the surface. As Ka pulled him up on the bank, fear seized Muku for a dreadful second. Suppose his beautiful coat had washed off in the water! No. When the pool settled again, the menehune reflected in it was still wearing hair. But now he looked as sleek as a seal with shining water drops dripping from his nose. At the sight, Muku shook himself merrily and laughed as heartily as the others at the joke.

The menehunes had a sport Muku loved. It was sliding on a ti leaf. A good tough ti leaf made a perfect sled, and there were always plenty of ti bushes to choose from. It was a long hard climb to the top of the slope where he loved to slide, but once there, a menehune could flash to the bottom like a falling star.

"The last one down is a cuckoo's egg!" Muku would shout. Then he would throw himself on his stomach and whizz from sight. Sometimes he would lie on his side and slide. But for real thrills, he liked to sit with his knees drawn up to his chest while he clutched the sides of the ti leaves with both hands. Soon he was the best slider of them all and never once was a cuckoo's egg.

Muku became a worker too. As his back grew stronger and the muscles of his arms and legs developed, he advanced from carrying pebbles to stones the size of goose eggs and sometimes bigger.

"Look at our little one," his mother often said to his sisters as they dug taro roots or collected sticks for the fire. "See how he helps with the building. His father is proud of him."

The sisters only grunted. They still resented their little brother. This didn't bother Muku at all, but something else did. Many times when the menehunes were trying desperately to finish their work, the sun would come up. The minute it did, they had to stop. "Pau," they would say, "It is finished," for never again could they return to what they had been making.

"Why do they say, 'Pau, it is finished' when it isn't finished?" Muku asked Ka one night.

"It is finished as far as they are concerned since they can't go back to it," Ka answered.

"But what good is half a wall? Or half a dam in a stream? Our work on such things is wasted."

Ka laughed. "Don't take it so hard, young fellow. Tomorrow night I will climb the mountain and catch the moon by her legs. Then I will keep her in the sky until our work is finished."

"Look at the boaster!" jeered the other menehunes. "Look at the master of the moon!"

Ka had only been fooling, but now he snapped back at them. "If you don't think I can do it, look at the sky tomorrow night. Maui bound the sun with a coconut rope when he wanted a longer day, and I will hang on to the moon until we have enough of the night. I swear it."

"Don't swear it, Ka!" Muku cried out in alarm. "Remember what must happen if you break your word. No one can do such an impossible thing!"

"I can, and I will," Ka answered stubbornly.

"Then I will go with you," declared Muku.

"No, no!" cried the others. "There may be danger, and you are the only son of our chief!"

But Nai-pu shook his head. "Let him go. The son of a chief must be prepared for danger."

So the next night, Ka rolled two shrimps and some sugar cane in a leaf for lunch, and he and Muku started to climb the steep cone of the mountain. Up, up, up, they toiled, often slipping and sliding and clutching at shrubs. Presently the valley fell below them, and the summit drew nearer and nearer. At last, puffing and panting, they reached the top and threw themselves down to rest. They had hardly done so, when over their heads they heard the sound of great whirring wings.

"Hide, Ka!" Muku gasped, diving into a thicket.

But before Ka could conceal himself, a huge owl spiraled down from the sky and settled on a rock directly in front of him. Ka stepped back in surprise and fear, shielding his head with his arm. But the owl made no move to attack. Glassy-eyed, Ka stared at her. The owl stared back, unblinking. This was the queen of the owls, who had come to shame him. The son of the chief was too frightened to breathe. "Run, Ka, run!" he wanted to shout, but no sound came from his throat. And Ka was powerless to tear his gaze from the owl.

Endless time dragged by. At any second, Muku expected that cruel beak to snap off Ka's head if the claws didn't seize him, or the wings sweep him over the cliff!

Frozen with fear, he watched from his shelter of leaves.

But the Owl Queen held Ka motionless with her yellow eyes alone. Not until the triumphant moon yawned and slid from the sky, did the great bird release him. Then she ruffled the feathers around her neck and hooted in derision.

"Boaster, boaster! Hoo, hoo, hoo! Now we'll see what happens to you!" Off she flew, brushing Ka to the ground with her wings.

Muku crawled out of his thicket. He was shivering for the first time in months, but not from cold. "Are you all right, Ka? I thought the owl would surely kill you, and I did nothing to save you. Oh, Ka, I am a coward!"

Ka shook his head. "We would both have died if you had tried, for then she would have attacked. Oh no, Muku. She came here to trick me, as the young owl tricked you. I have been forced to break my word, and now I shall be turned to stone."

"No, Ka, no!" Muku cried, for he loved the jolly boaster.

But Ka answered, "It must be so. I failed my oath."

As he spoke, the first of his people came scrambling to the mountain top, closely followed by Chief Nai-pu and the others. Not a word did they say as they formed a ring around Ka. There were tears in their eyes as they pointed the finger of shame. Sadly, Nai-pu chanted the ancient curse.

He who fails his word
Alone
Must remain,
Eternal stone.

As the chant ended, Ka fell to the ground, and the next minute a smooth black stone lay in his place. Muku threw himself upon it and wept. But when the workers sought to roll the stone down to the sea, as was the custom, Nai-pu waved them aside.

"Let him stay where he is. What he tried to do would have helped us all. But for the Queen Owl, he might have succeeded. His curse will be to look forever at the moon, who still comes and goes as she pleases."

In this way was Ka punished. But many a night, Muku crept away from the workers and climbed to the top of the mountain. Here he would sit and talk to his friend the black stone.

8.
Laka
and the
Moon Tree

THE FATE OF KA made the owls sworn enemies of the menehunes. Often, concealed in her nest, Mimo heard them plotting to drive the little people from the island. King Owl had long since lined his nest with Muku's tapa jacket, and now that their queen had caused the death of Ka, there was no living with them.

"We must surely do battle with these savage creatures," Nai-pu said at last. "But first we must build two dams. I promised them long ago to Al-e-ko-ko and his sister Ka-la. When I was very young, these humans saved me from the clutches of a hawk. I could not reward them then. But now I have learned they need dams, and these must be the best we can build."

So the menehunes set to work to collect the finest stones, but Nai-pu rejected so many that the work lagged.

One night, when the moon made shining ribbons of the cascades they planned to restrain, crackling twigs warned of strangers approaching. Swiftly, the menehunes scurried from sight as a boy and an old woman made their way through a tangle of vines. But Mimo flew after them from tree to tree, and Muku followed like a lizard in the grass.

"I will never return to our home until I have a canoe, Grandmother," the boy was saying. "You know I must seek my parents."

"No craft can take you to them, Laka. They sailed far away when you were a baby. I have told you that a hundred times. Give up this wild notion."

The boy shook his head. "Say what you will, I must seek them, either in a fine canoe that will skim the waves or in some old dugout half sunk in the water."

His grandmother sighed. "If you must go, look for a tree with leaves shaped like the new moon. Build your canoe from that. I shall return to our home and wait for you."

So they parted, and Muku and Mimo had only the tall lad to follow. The fragrance of jasmine was heavy on the air as he went deeper and deeper into the forest. But nowhere could he find the tree with the moon-shaped leaves. At last Muku whispered to Mimo.

"Let us show him the tree, Mimo. When he cuts it down, he is sure to find it too heavy to carry, and our people can take it. With his help we will hasten the work on the dams."

"How clever of you, Muku! I shall call to him from its branches. Then he can't possibly miss it."

Off she flew, urging Laka with bird notes to follow. She finished her song in the moon tree. When he saw that, Laka began to chop it down. But his ax was small, and the tree was stout. By the time it came crashing to the ground, the night was almost over, and he was very tired.

"I'll leave it here until tomorrow," he said to himself. "Then I'll come back and strip off the branches and drag my fine tree to the seashore. There I shall make my canoe."

So he marked the spot and went home to sleep. As soon as he was out of sight, Muku whistled to the other menehunes and a swarm of them whisked the tree off to the dam site.

"Just wait until Laka comes back," chuckled Muku. "I want to be here to see him!"

With the evening, Laka returned to look for his tree. Chopping it down had made him so tired he had slept through the whole day. But what had become of it?

47

Only a handful of chips remained where it had fallen! Peeking through the leaves, Muku felt almost sorry as he watched the boy's bewilderment. Suddenly the sweet trill of bird notes brightened the forest, and Laka went in pursuit of it. This time, Muku laughed in his throat for Mimo had perched in a second tree.

Once again Laka set to work with his little ax, and once again a silvery tree crashed to the ground. Laka tried his best to carry it away, but he was just too tired. So, he marked the spot with special care and made off through the forest. The menehunes had barely time to carry the tree away before the sun came blazing into the heavens. Nai-pu laughed until he shook when he saw it.

"Who says I haven't a clever son?" he roared. "You people may have the muscles, but he has the brains!"

The third night Laka came again, and for the third time Mimo sent her sweetest notes from a tree with moon-shaped leaves. But this one was so tall and strong that Laka was still chopping away at it when daylight came.

"Well," said Muku confidently, "we know where the tree is, and certainly if Laka couldn't carry the smaller ones away, we have no need to fear for this." So he trailed home after the other menehunes to sleep through the day.

When the fourth evening came, the menehunes swiftly gathered around the fallen tree to hurry it out of sight before the boy could return. There it lay as he had left it, wrapped in its shining leaves. Countless little hands lifted it from the ground. But just as they had it clear of its resting place, Laka himself sprang up from a trench he had dug beneath it and rushed wildly at them. Away sped the menehunes like shadows. All but one. He was left struggling frantically in Laka's strong hands. It was Muku.

9. The Magic Canoe

LAKA SAT DOWN ON A STONE and examined Muku. He thought he had never seen anything so strange as this wriggling little creature. And Muku thought he had never seen so huge a hand.

"You don't look very tempting," said Laka at last, "but I suppose I must eat you. I don't see anything else around and I'm hungry."

"Oh please, not that!" screamed Muku in terror.

"First I will have to skin you," continued Laka as though he had not heard, "and then I'll stuff you with a few squid and bake you in my grandmother's oven."

"Oh no!" squealed Muku.

"Or broil you with bananas."

"No, no!" howled his victim.

"Or even simmer you in coconut milk."

"Don't do it, don't do it!" implored poor Muku, weak from fright. "I'm not young and tender as you think. I am really old and tough!"

"My grandmother could rub you with papaya juice. That will make an owl fit to eat," murmured Laka, as though he was talking to himself.

At this suggestion, Muku could only shiver in terror. His teeth were chattering so violently he could say nothing.

Then Laka laughed cheerfully and settled Muku more comfortably on his knee. "Oh stop howling. I wouldn't eat you if I were starving. Besides my grandmother has pork lau-lau for supper. But what do you people mean by stealing my trees?"

"We only did it so that we can get the dams built in a hurry. Once we start, we must finish them both in a night." Then he told Laka about Nai-pu's debt to Al-e-ko-ko and Ka-la and why the menehunes had to fight the owls.

"I hope your side wins," said Laka when he had finished. "But I am afraid you won't be there to help them unless you can do something about my canoe."

"We will," Muku promised. "You can have it before this night is over if you will just let me whistle."

"All right," agreed Laka, loosening his grip on Muku's

arms but holding fast to his legs. "Only don't try any tricks. And, mind, I don't want that canoe stranded here in the forest. You must carry it down to the water."

"We will," Muku assured him.

"Don't forget that a canoe needs paddles and an outrigger. And what is more, I don't want it half-finished. If you can't complete my canoe and launch it, I won't let you whistle."

"It shall be finished and launched."

"Then whistle!"

Muku put his fingers to his lips and whistled. The next minute there was a great rustling of leaves and crackling of branches as hundreds of menehunes rushed to the scene. But when Muku told them of his promise to Laka, some of them turned away angrily.

"Why should we delay the work on the dams because you were clumsy and got caught?" demanded one.

Muku hopped up on the stump and answered him sternly. "I am the son of Nai-pu, your chief, and I have given my word. Laka has cut down three trees for us, and the least we can do is to build his canoe. Now get to work!"

Nai-pu had remained in the background, but as Muku spoke he nodded approvingly. "You heard him," he shouted, "Get to work!"

As the menehunes set upon it, the moon tree slid from its bark like a hand from a glove. With flashing axes they split the naked trunk lengthwise and sent up a shower of chips from its heart. Swiftly they hollowed it out. Soon the curve of the prow appeared. Laka watched in fascination as they smoothed the sides and shaped the stern. Half of the company fashioned the outrigger. Others wove straw into sails. While they labored, the moon vanished for a moment behind a cloud. When it reappeared, the canoe was finished.

"Don't forget the paddles!" called Laka.

Even as he spoke, a slender bough seemed to leap into the air unaided. There it spun violently for a moment before it settled into the canoe, a perfect paddle. Then a second crossed that and rested its delicate tip on the ribs at the bottom. Complete and flawless, the trim craft rose through the air as if on wings. Laka thought it was sailing away by itself and plunged after it. Then he

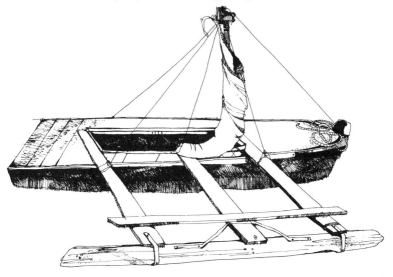

realized what was happening. The menehunes concealed beneath it were simply carrying the canoe to the ocean as they had promised. Checking his wild dash, he looked around for Muku. But Muku, still aching in his arms and legs, had hidden behind a scarlet hibiscus bush.

"Where are you, Muku?" Laka shouted. "Come sail with me in my canoe. It's the most beautiful boat in the world."

"No thank you," replied Muku in a voice Laka couldn't locate, "I've spent time enough with you. My legs will be stiff for a month!"

"I'm sorry about that. You have carried out your bargain faithfully, and if ever I can do anything to help you, let me know."

"You will probably have more than one chance to do that!" twittered Mimo from a monkeypod tree.

"Thank you, Laka," an invisible Muku replied politely. "I won't forget." Then, as Laka's brown legs disappeared from sight, he gave a deep sigh of relief. "My adventure has ended happily after all," he said to Mimo.

Mimo sniffed. "I'm not so sure of that. I wonder what the owls were doing while we took time off to build a canoe."

Muku squirmed at the thought. For all her virtues, Mimo could certainly take the fun out of things.

10. Caught in the Shark Trap

As Muku trudged through the forest after Mimo, he paused for a moment at the edge of a steep cliff. Far below, the waves feathered the beach with foam.

"Step back," warned Mimo. "You're too near the edge!"

But before Muku could obey her, the earth had crumbled beneath him and the next second he was whirling through space. Down he sped through the empty air, spinning round and round like a ku-ku-i nut top. At last he landed with such a thump that every bit of breath was knocked out of him. When his senses came back, and he tried to sit up, he found he couldn't stir. A net of vines held him flat on his back. Then he realized what had happened to him. It was low tide, and he had fallen into a trap made of morning-glory vines which his people had set for a shark. No matter how frantically he struggled, the vines held him fast.

Suddenly there was a whirring of wings over his head, and Mimo alighted on his chest. "If I ever saw an unlucky menehune," she chirped angrily, "you are it!"

"Oh don't, Mimo," Muku moaned.

"Two traps in one night! You must surely have set a new record!"

"Get me out of here, Mimo," Muku cried, now really frightened. "The shark may come any minute!"

Mimo cocked her head scornfully. "I suppose you think he will swim in beside you. Don't worry. A shark has better sense!"

Nevertheless she set to work with her sharp beak, snapping and tugging at the tough vines. Then she too became frightened, for nothing she could do would tear open the trap.

"I will have to get help," she said at last, trying to be calm.

"Oh don't leave me to the shark!"

"Even if he should come, you are safe from him there."

"He could swallow me, net and all!" sobbed poor Muku. As Mimo pictured the huge jaws of the shark, she knew that he could.

Suddenly Muku gave a shout, this time for joy. "Laka,"

he exclaimed. "Find Laka. He said he would help me if I needed him. He must be near by, and he can save me!"

Off flew Mimo at top speed to find Laka. She had no trouble at all, for he was paddling his canoe not far from shore. The moment he heard what had happened, he sped to the rescue. As he did so, the shark, who had been quietly dozing in a tangle of seaweed, discovered the lad.

"Man," said the shark to himself. "There is nothing tastier than a man. Why should I waste my time eating fish!" With that thought, he turned around and swiftly glided after the canoe.

Laka was skimming the waves like a ripple, but with the merest flip of his tail, the shark shot ahead. His stony little eyes glinted hungrily in the moonlight. Laka

caught one glimpse of that sinister shape and paddled desperately. To Mimo, perched on his shoulder, it seemed that the beach was rushing to meet them. She even thought she could see Muku's head bobbing in the trap where the water was shallowest.

Suddenly, as they neared the shore, the shark veered from his course. With horrified eyes, Laka saw the huge gray body lunge at him as though heaved up from the ocean floor. He tried frantically to turn his canoe. But the thrust of the shark rushing by him had torn away the outrigger, and the canoe seemed to spin in a whirlpool. Over the side plunged Laka like a stone shot from a sling. Down, down, down he went. As the water closed over his head, he snatched from his belt the little ax which had felled the moon trees.

Now the shark was upon him. With one disdainful flip of his tail, he swept past the canoe to seek out its owner. As he spied the slender brown figure, he bared his teeth and charged. Just as he opened his cavernous jaws, Laka swam beneath him and drew a long gash through his side. The wounded monster whipped around like a coiled

spring and lunged at his enemy. But once again Laka swerved from his path and drew the blade of his ax through the thick flesh. Hovering over the jagged black rocks, lacy with foam, Mimo watched the struggle in horror until the churning and heaving of the maddened shark hid the pair from her sight. Unnoticed, the splintered prow of the forgotten canoe scraped on the shore.

But at last the frightful boiling of the water stopped. Then, in a widening stain, a body arose — the battered hulk of the shark. Now those hungry jaws were closed, and the vicious tail had stopped its wild threshing. Only the cold little eyes still gleamed in the moonlight. The shark was **dead**.

Laka floated into shore on his back. He felt so beaten and bruised that he feared every bone in his body was broken. But when he moved his arms, his hands and his fingers responded stiffly and he discovered that he could still kick. At last he felt the sugary sand of the beach beneath his shoulders, and exhausted, he managed to crawl up on it. It was then that he realized that he had lost his ax to the shark. No matter. It had saved his life. His canoe lay an arm's length from him on its one good side. Bits of the shattered outrigger still clung to the other. Laka looked at it bitterly.

"That's what I get for trying to help a menehune," he told himself.

But the thought came to him that only for the work of these little men he might never have had such a canoe; and for the first time since his encounter with the shark, he remembered Muku's plight. No hurry now. The shark could harm no one. He closed his eyes weakly.

"I must rest a minute," he thought.

A light touch on his arm woke him up. Muku was standing beside him. Laka drew himself up on his elbow. He could hardly believe his eyes.

"I thought. . . How did you get out of the trap?"

Muku hung his head. "My people came for me," he confessed.

Laka looked at him angrily. "If they could do that without any help from me, why didn't you send for them in the first place?"

"I was afraid I would be punished," Muku admitted shamefacedly. "First I let *you* catch me, and then I fell into the shark trap all in one night."

"Do you realize that I nearly paid with my life for your carelessness? And what about my canoe? Its outrigger is in splinters, and the paddles are lost. I can't even get home!"

"Oh I can fix that," Muku assured him with relief. "But you can never go back to your grandmother. The moon-tree canoe will take you to a far shore where your parents are waiting for you."

Laka shrugged. "Far shore, indeed! That poor thing will sink if I put a toe in it!" He turned his eyes to the spot where his ruined canoe had rested. Then he sat bolt upright in astonishment. For there, trim and fit, the little craft danced at anchor with two paddles crossed in its stern. A length of morning-glory vine secured it to a jagged rock. For a bewildered minute Laka looked at the sight. Then he rubbed his eyes and looked again.

"How long was I asleep?" he asked. But when he turned to Muku for an answer, the beach was bare. Only a hermit crab shared it with him and his canoe.

11.
The Battle with the Owls

AT LAST THE NIGHT CAME when the menehunes were finally ready to build the twin dams for Al-e-ko-ko and his sister Ka-la. Near the cascades, heaps of stones stood in readiness beside Laka's two trees. As the workers waited restlessly for the moon to rise, brittle twigs snapped spitefully under foot, and banana trees rattled dry leaves. No rain had fallen in so long a time that the brooks were silent, and hills and valleys lay parched and stricken. The cascades themselves seemed hardly worth damming up, reduced as they were to a trickle.

In the stone basin before Nai-pu's grass house, the fire had burned to a single log for in the great heat no one wanted to tend it. But Mimo had more than the heat to bother her, and so, she thought, had the menehunes. Hidden from sight in a koa tree, she had overheard the owls plotting. As soon as it was safe, she flew to Chief Nai-pu.

"The owls are gathering from throughout the grove, Father. Look in the trees and you will see them. There are so many of them that the weight of their bodies bends down the branches. They may attack at any moment!"

"They wouldn't dare do that," answered Nai-pu, fanning himself with a palm leaf. "They fight only with threats and tricks."

"Oh Father, be warned! They are only biding their time. What shall we do if they swoop down upon us?"

"I tell you they won't! First we must build the dams. Then we can worry about the owls."

With every feather angrily ruffled, Mimo flew off to Muku. "The owls aren't going to wait until we are ready for them, but our father thinks they will!"

"What can we do? The dams have to be built; we have promised. We must think of some way to alert the workers if the attack comes while they're busy."

Mimo snapped at a moth. "Any suggestions?"

"We must go to Ka. He may be a stone, but from his mountain top he sees what is going on and perhaps he can think of a scheme."

"Let us go quickly then. There is no time to lose. It's a pity you are too big now to ride on my back!"

Off she skimmed through the trees. Muku ran after her, slipping and sliding through the matted vines that clung to the slope. The thought that for once he was too big for something helped him to hurry.

When he reached the spot where Ka lay, the moon was already shining on his old friend, and Mimo was perched beside him.

"Ka," Muku whispered with his cheek pressed to the black stone, "how can we defend ourselves against the owls?"

In a voice so low they could hardly hear him, Ka answered, "Mimo must ask Chief Nai-pu for the favor he promised when she brought him the fire-stick. Then do as I tell you."

"What favor shall I ask?" Mimo chirped.

"Listen carefully." Then Ka revealed his plan on which the lives of all depended. "You must make no mistake, for you will have no chance to correct it after the dams are started. Are you sure you know just what to do?"

"Oh yes!" they assured him.

"Then be off! Be off!"

The menehunes were awaiting Nai-pu's signal to start work as Mimo alighted on his upraised arm.

"Wait, Father, wait!" she gasped breathlessly. "I must have the favor you promised me!"

Nai-pu shook her off impatiently. "Not now, not now! Can't you see I am busy?"

"Please, please, Father. Listen! This is ever so important!"

"Ask it quickly then," Nai-pu snapped. "The moon has risen and we have no time to waste! If you have just decided to become one of us again. . ."

"Oh no. Something quite different. I want everyone here to pick two big ti leaves."

Nai-pu stared at her. "Ti leaves! Now?"

"Please! You must trust me. Everyone. . . *two!*"

Nai-pu shook his head in bewilderment, but he barked out an order. Instantly, the menehunes rushed to strip the ti bushes. At that moment Muku arrived, panting. He tugged at Mimo's wing.

"Remember, two piles at the edge of the cliff!"

"Two piles at the edge of the cliff," she directed the workers.

They followed instructions until they had two towering piles of thick shining ti leaves. "Pau. It is finished," they grunted.

"Then start the dams!" commanded Nai-pu.

At his signal, the menehunes snatched up the stones from the store they had so long collected. From hand to hand the stones flashed, each one set to perfection.

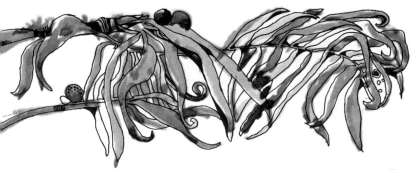

Swiftly and silently the dam rose. Al-e-ko-ko's was finished. The moon watched as they started the second.
Then, without warning, such a soul-chilling screech arose
from the treetops that the workers froze in their places.
The owls were attacking! Down they plunged, owls by
the thousands, beating their wings in a murderous fury.
With claws bared and yellow eyes flashing, they swooped
on their terrified victims.

The menehunes fled in frantic confusion, straight to
the edge of the cliff. But there, ready and waiting, were
Muku and Mimo. . . and there were the towers of leaves.

"Slide," screamed Muku, "Slide on the ti leaves!"

"Slide on your stomachs!" shrilled Mimo.

"Pau!" cried the first workers. "Pau!" cried the others.
Snatching up the leathery leaves, they threw themselves
over the cliff. Some of them sped down the slope straight
as arrows. Some went careening and skidding like stones.
But from under the very beaks of the hoot owls, they
flashed out of sight in a landslide of leaves.

The owls screamed with rage as they saw themselves
cheated of victory, for bound by their pledge never to

leave their grove, they could only snap at heads that flashed by and try to hold back the others.

"Beat them off!" shouted Muku, as Nai-pu and those who stood by him grabbed up the ti leaves for weapons and shields. Again and again they beat back the enraged owls until the tough leaves were tattered and riddled with holes. But by this time most of the workers were safe from their beaks.

"Come, Muku!" cried Nai-pu, and followed the others. But as Muku started to obey, Mimo shrieked, "We have forgotten the fire-stick! I must go back to get it. Slide, Muku, slide!"

Only one ti leaf was left whole on the ground. Thankfully, Muku stooped to snatch it up. But before his fingers could touch it, a rush of angry wings swept by him, and away flew the leaf in the beak of an owl, the very owl who had stolen his coat!

Around and around he flew in dizzying circles, slashing at Muku's head with the last of the leaves. As Muku shrank back from the vicious attack, he saw at his feet the remains of his shield. So little was left in one piece! Could he possibly slide down on that scrap of a leaf? The owl swooped down at him again, but he ducked, protecting his eyes with his arm. As the bird's wings brushed the top of Muku's head, he snatched up the leaf and edged to the brink of the cliff. Then he squatted down and squeezed his knees up under his chin. That way, he could just fit on the leaf. How wonderful to be small after all!

The owl saw Muku's plan, and his yellow eyes glistened. Now was the time to finish the menehune off! But before he could pounce, a horrified squawk came from high above as the fire-stick fell from Mimo's scorched beak! Down streaked the flame like the tail of a comet and buried itself in the owl's ruffled feathers. Caught in mid-air, the bird wheeled, screaming with terror, and flew through the forest with plumage ablaze.

Then out of the sky dropped Mimo, crying, "Slide, Muku, slide! The mountain's on fire!"

"Fly with me, Mimo," her brother called back, as clinging with both hands to his bit of a leaf, he vanished from sight.

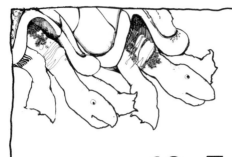

12. Escape from the Island

BELOW IN THE VALLEY, the menehunes were safe from the owls, but they crowded the beach in a miserable huddle. Almost everyone was scratched and bruised, and many a tuft of hair had been torn from their skins.

"My back is broken!" cried Nai-pu. He had slipped from his ti leaf and rolled half the way down.

"My stomach is skinned," groaned an unhappy worker. But the others were too concerned with their own aching bones to pay any attention.

Suddenly, forgetting his broken back, Nai-pu leaped to his feet. "Where's Muku?" he shouted, "Where's Mimo?"

The words were hardly out of his mouth, when Muku, still clinging to his wisp of a leaf, slid into sight. Mimo flew over his head.

With a cry of relief, Nai-pu seized his son in his arms.

Then he held up a finger for Mimo to perch on. "Brave children," he said, "we all owe you our lives!"

"Oh no, Father," moaned Mimo through her charred beak, "I dropped the fire-stick, and the island will soon be in flames!"

"It had burned to the end," cried Muku. "She had held it as long as she could. Besides it fell on the owl that was attacking me."

Nai-pu looked from his son and daughter to the fire sweeping through the dry trees. "I know you did your best, Mimo. We've escaped the owls, but now it seems we must perish in the fire!"

"Wait, Father," exclaimed Muku. "Whatever our fate, Ka must share it. He made the plan to slide down from the cliff. We can't leave him there on the mountain alone!"

Nai-pu frowned. Save Ka who had disgraced him before the owls? As he hesitated, a great cloud of smoke billowed down from the mountain. The menehunes clustered about him in terror.

"Save us, Chief Nai-pu! Tell us what we must do!"

Nai-pu was helpless. But Mimo called to Muku, "Throw the pebbles into the water. Call Tina."

Tina? The pebbles? Then Muku remembered what Tina had told him when the owl stole his coat. "Throw three pebbles into the water, and I will help you. Throw five, and all my turtle brothers and sisters will come!" This was certainly the time for five!

Hardly had the fifth pebble splashed, when the sea began to churn strangely. The next minute, thousands of turtles swam to the shore. They were lined up so closely their backs made a pavement. The menehunes stared open-mouthed as one of their number crawled up on the beach. It was Tina.

"Save us, my daughter!" cried Nai-pu.

Tina looked at him proudly. "What can a turtle do for a chief?"

"I will make you a menehune again," Nai-pu offered.

Tina shook her head. "No thank you, Father. I am content and much safer in my shell."

Muku leaned down and patted her. "Oh Tina, you came as you promised. I know you will save us!"

Tina nodded. "But first I must ask a favor."

"Ask *any* favor. I promise to grant it," Nai-pu declared, bending over her.

"Bring Ka back to this company and you shall go to Kauai on the backs of my friends. You'll be safe on a beautiful island."

Then all the menehunes shouted, "Bring back Ka!"

"It shall be done," agreed Nai-pu. Standing tall on the

beach in the ruddy light, he clapped his hands until the echoes clapped back. Every head was turned to the mountain.

Suddenly, from high up above them, through the dense screen of smoke and pillars of fire, a black stone came crashing and plunging, straight to the spot where the whole company stood. Nai-pu touched it with his finger tips.

"Return to us, Ka-u-ki-u-ki. All has been forgiven."

At his words, the black stone vanished, and Ka sprang up, hearty and smiling. "Thank you, Chief Nai-pu. Thank you Muku, Mimo, and Tina. You will never regret my return to this company."

With a shout of delight, Muku threw his arms around his old friend and hugged him. The others cheered in approval. Suddenly Muku had a dreadful thought.

"Oh Ka, the island is burning. We set it afire. Who will save the poor humans?"

Ka patted his shoulder. "Don't worry, Muku. The fire will not spread to the valley, and there they will be safe."

"How do you know?"

The rumble of thunder answered his question.

"Hurry now," cried Tina. "My companions are waiting!"

Slipping and splashing, the menehunes waded into the water and climbed on the backs of the turtles. Mimo flew over their heads. Perched on his father's shoulder, Muku blew a clinging owl feather into the air and waved his aloha to the island.

DATE DUE

MAY 4 1981	Joson Rick	7-D
	Le	9-D
	Ruc	
	Kerry	8-D